If in doubt —
follow your nose.

Max +.

I, NERD

A novelette

MAX SYDNEY SMITH

OPEN PEN

First Published in 2022
by Open Pen, 25 Crescent Road, London, E13 0LU
First Edition
openpen.co.uk
9781916413672
OPNOV012

OPEN PEN NOVELETTES #10
"I, Nerd"
© Max Sydney Smith 2022

Cover illustration by Pierre Buttin - pierrebuttin.com
© Pierre Buttin 2022

For Ralph,
brother and nerd-in-arms since Sixth Edition.

THE GAME

It seems everyone knows why I play the Game except me. My brother says it is because I am sexually repressed. My sister says it is because I have an obsessive, hoarding mentality. My father will change the subject whenever it comes up but I know he thinks the desire to collect things stems from unresolved toilet training conflict. And my mother says it is because I have good attention to detail.

I play every Sunday at a club on the top floor of a converted warehouse. On the ground floor is a hipster bar. I have to walk through the smoking area to get to the stairs that go up to the club. Mostly in the winter it is all right, though I can always see the hipsters watching me from inside. They sit on bar stools at the window counter, the men with beanies perched uselessly over their ears and the women curling the ends of their hair over fingers tattooed with geometric shapes. They cradle mulled wine, smoked porters, or whatever else it is they like drinking.

But today the bar is holding a winter festival. There is a queue of bodies packed into the side alley leading to the warehouse and I have to turn my case full of carefully wrapped miniatures sideways to fit past them, their sharp elbows like a bristling forest of spears.

When I reach the front of the queue I mumble an explanation to the security guard that I am here for the games club upstairs. They have put sound systems out on the canal side terrace and it is loud.

The security guard cups his hand behind his ear.

'The games club.' I am clutching my miniature case close to my chest with both hands so I can only nod my chin in the direction of the stairs.

After he has let me through, smirking, and I have trudged up the first, second and third flight of stairs and pushed open the heavy double doors of the club and they have closed behind me, the music and chatter from the bar drops away.

It takes a few seconds to adjust to the darkness of the club. There are big windows all along the front wall but the blinds are half drawn. The owner is behind the bar. It is always the owner behind the bar. I do not know if it is because he is the only one who works here or if he can never get anyone to work on a Sunday. He is a short man from Taunton who wears fleeces in earthy colours and ties his hair in a ponytail.

He starts pouring me a beer and cracks a joke about starting early. He makes it every week and I always say, 'It's never too early' and he laughs and the two hobby painters standing at the bar laugh and then we are quiet.

The hobby painters are older men with grey crew cuts. They divide their time between standing at the bar, smoking cigarettes on the balcony at the back of the club and assembling and painting miniatures on one of the small tables. They have small rucksacks from which they produce an endless parade of unpainted miniatures, pliers, files, brushes, wet palettes and pots of paint.

I take the beer and make my way slowly across the room to our table. It is a big room. Along the back wall is metal shelving with every kind of board game you can imagine and in front of the shelves are a few small tables surrounded by sofas and armchairs. In the early evening these tables fill up with casual gamers who come to play Catan, Risk or other games that only take a couple of hours to play.

But most of the room is taken up by five large tables, lit by low hanging snooker hall lamps. It is more or less the same people on these tables every Sunday. Two smartly dressed men are already measuring out cannon ranges for a Napoleonic wargame on the first table. On the second, a few teenagers are setting up a cyberpunk skirmish game. The third table is reserved for a rolling crowd of Japanese students who play Magic the Gathering and the fourth table for a group of big bearded men who play Dungeons and Dragons but neither of these groups have arrived yet. In the far corner is our table, and we play the Game.

There are two types of people who play the Game: the Gamers and the Hobbyists. The Hobbyists say the Gamers are all crunch and no fluff and the Gamers say the Hobbyists are all fluff and no crunch.

The Gamers are mostly interested in playing the Game. They would be quite happy to turn up to the club with bits of A4 paper cut to various unit sizes and with the names of the units written on them in biro. Some of them would even prefer it, because they can write unit stats on the paper for reference and the paper is easier to pivot and move than a ten by eight centimetre rectangle of MDF glued with twenty Winged Fiend miniatures. They get their kicks from turning over tactics and strategies and coming up with different ways to break the crunch of the game mechanics. It is the Gamers who go to the national tournaments and it is because they are always poking and tinkering under the bonnet of the rules that the game designers on the Rules Committee are constantly releasing amendments and new editions and so the internal equilibrium between the different armies is maintained. The Hobbyists usually refer to the army lists of the Gamers as filthy, hyper-competitive and unrealistic. Simon is definitely a Gamer and will get into an argument every week for trying to use some new rules clarification he read about on one of the community forums to his advantage. He usually wins, partly because he is technically right but also because the twin who is Games Master thinks of him as his protégé.

The Hobbyists are mostly interested in collecting and painting miniatures. They buy models they like the look of regardless of how good the stats are and spend months painting them. Their miniatures are positioned in dynamic poses and the bases are decorated with small trees, glassy rivers or towers crawling with threadlike ivy vines. They get their kick out of inventing narratives to fluff out these tableaux. Each of their units has a backstory and they can recite the lineage of their heroes for several generations. Jonathan is a Hobbyist. He retypes his army list every week, substituting the official names from the online army list builder for custom ones he has invented. So instead of Dwarf Shieldwall company it will say Brodrick, Son of Brawnshort, and the Shieldwall of Stoneguard. This kind of thing drives the Gamers mad because, they say, it is impossible to tell at a glance what is what. One time Simon really flew off the handle at Jonathan about that Dwarf Shieldwall company and since then we all agreed that Jonathan had to write out both the official name and his own for every unit, although he still puts his name first, and in bold.

Sometimes a Hobbyist will refuse to play a Gamer because the latter has substituted several units for rectangles of cardboard, each with a different Early Learning Centre plastic farm animal tacked onto it. 'You're just scared you're gonna lose,' retort the Gamers. And they flap their elbows and coo, 'Chicken! Chicken!' Then the Hobbyists are angry in a quiet, deeply private way and the twin who is Games Master has to call us back from our tables and generate new random integers on his phone until everyone is happy with their match partner.

It is true that the Hobbyists always lose to the Gamers. It happens every week and every time the Hobbyists get salty and swear this really is the final straw and next week they are going to turn up with the filthiest list imaginable. But they always turn up the following week with at least one unit they have only brought because they have just finished painting it and another that looks good beside it from a colour perspective and so they lose all over again.

When I get to our corner table I can see that Dave has finished painting and basing his Landsknechte army. He has been working on it for the best part of a year. Dave is a Hobbyist who collects historical miniatures and in the Game he plays as Humans. He has a wife and kids, but he rarely talks about them. Mostly he talks about the pike and shot era and the ins and outs of military history through the Middle Ages.

'Robin! There you are.' Dave claps me on the back and gestures with his other hand towards the table. 'Will you look at them.'

They do look impressive. I ask if it is okay to touch them and he tells me it is, as long as I hold them by the bases.

I pick up a unit at random and turn it this way and that under the low hanging lamp. 'The yellow really does pop,' I say. He has layered the arquebusier's jackets with three different yellow paints and an ochre wash. Every sleeve, pocket, cuff and collar is perfect.

But at the same time my body surges with envy. I want to have done that. I start searching for things Dave must have sacrificed to have had time to do this. What a loser, I think, already feeling guilty for thinking it.

We are all losers of a sort. One time when I was reading on the bus home from school, a boy on the seat in front of me leant back and snatched the book from my hands. 'You reading about wizards and shit again?' When I did not answer he threw it back to me. The other boys at the back of the bus were half watching. He looked at them, then back at me. 'Who would win in a fight between Merlin and Gandalf?' The other boys were staring now, ready to laugh.

I looked up at the boy. 'I don't know.'

He would not let it go. 'Who would win? Come on!'

Reluctantly, I considered the question. I pushed my glasses up the bridge of my nose. 'It's complicated. They're from two different worlds.'

At this the boy laughed and turned to the others and they laughed, big baboonish peals of laughter. 'He fucking answered it. Did you hear, he fucking answered it!' One of the others said, 'It's not real you freak!'

I was squeezing my legs together and arms together as if I was trying to occupy as small a space as possible. But in some far back part of my mind I was also thinking that what was real was actually very subjective.

It happened to all of us. Simon used to be pushed off the bus three stops early and have to walk home in the rain. Some kids fired rubber pellets at Bryce's head back in Durban. And Dave told us there was a group of lads who once threw a rubbish bin at him when he was on his bike and a few times egged his house. That was the eighties for you, he grinned.

It is because we were bullied for being nerds that we hold the things we were bullied for so closely. These stories about wizards and Jedi, these worlds with magic and force fields, they are meaningful to us because we have suffered for them, because they were the cause and relief of our suffering.

I try not to remember the times when the shoe was on the other foot. That time in Year Five when the whole class sprang on Marcus Williams, who everyone hated because he was small and mouse-like and had dandruff. We pushed him under a table, closed the sides in with turned-over chairs, and kicked and hammered on the surfaces of the cage we had made for him. I try not to remember how victorious I felt when I looked from side to side as I hammered the chair seat and thought, I am one of them now, they have let me in, I am normal.

I am unpacking my miniatures when the twins arrive. I can hear them arguing as they pick their way between the tables towards me. The twins are as different as fire and water but they have the same blonde hair with the same side parting and wear the same style of blue jeans and plain pastel shirts so I am always getting them mixed up. Or, I got them mixed up at first and now I have overthought it so much that I never know if my distinction is the initial, mixed-up distinction or the later, corrected one.

Each time I go to the club I think this time I will not get the twins mixed up. It is only ever a problem until they start taking out their armies and then I know, because one collects Elves and the other collects Undead. One will remove from his miniature case small bands of chariots pulled by white steeds and phalanxes of slender spearmen wearing silver chainmail and sea blue cloaks. And the other will put on the table legions of zombies, their skin rotting and weapons rusted, and their bases decorated with the desecrated ruins of cities.

Also the way one talks about women is not the way the other talks about women. The one who collects Elves and whose girlfriend is pregnant might say, 'My partner and I made black bean risotto last night, I never knew you could use red wine,' to which the other will roll his eyes and shake his hand as if giving the air a handjob. While twin who collects Undead might say, 'Man I just wish she was more of a slut and let me come over her tits you know,' to which his brother will sigh and close his eyes with a pained look on his face.

Mostly he does not speak, the twin who collects Elves, when his brother speaks like this. But today he must have said something particularly unpleasant because when they get to our table, the twin who collects Elves throws his coat on the chair and rounds on the other twin, saying, 'Why are you so fucking basic man?' The twin who collects Undead dismisses him with a wave of the hand, calling his brother a faggot and a white knight, and from there the exchange descends into a duel of expletives and then a stilted silence.

I keep my head down and concentrate on unpacking my miniatures. After a while one of the twins storms to the bar and the other sits across the table from me and lets out a groan of exasperation. I am so nervous about which one it is that I do not know what to say, because the kind of thing I might say to one is different to what I might say to the other as if I have two twin versions of myself inside me.

'They are closing the club,' the twin who collects Elves says. I can tell it is him because he has opened his case and I can see the ranks of spearmen resting on the bubble wrap, their pennants painted with elvish runes. Simon has arrived and the three of us are rolling the PVC mats out across the table.

I ask what he is talking about and he says again, 'They are closing the club. In June.' The twin who collects Elves helps the owner run the club membership scheme. He looks tired.

'Fuck. Why?' Simon says.

The twin who collects Elves shrugs. 'I think this whole street of warehouses is being turned into flats.'

Dave comes back from chatting to the hobby painters at the bar. He cradles his coffee in his hands and watches us adjust the mats so they are flush with the edge of the table. 'Oh that's a shame,' he says when the twin tells him. But he does not sound too upset.

Dave does not care where he plays. He has a car and does not pay much attention to other people. When the club closes he will play in a church hall or the backroom of a pub or his garage. But I do not have a garage and I do not want to play in any of those other places. We cannot play in a pub with everyone staring and smirking, or in a church hall, with some old person asking if we are playing toy soldiers. No, we play in the club because it is away from everyone, it is sealed off from the world by its three flights of stairs and heavy double doors.

Bryce and the twin who collects Undead come back with the scenery. The club keeps boxes of miniature terrain pieces labelled Historical Fantasy, Napoleonic, Cyberpunk, Grimdark.

'The bar downstairs is reopening round the corner,' Bryce says when he hears what we are talking about. Bryce is thin and ripped and covered in tattoos and spends three months a year in South Africa with his brother. He is obviously the best looking of us but none of us would ever acknowledge this. He works in a pizzeria nearby and knows everything about what is happening in the area.

'Yeah so we've actually reached an agreement with them,' the twin who collects Elves says. 'It's going to be a split level bar and they're going to put in a few big tables upstairs. So we're telling people they can play there.'

'We'd have the top floor?' I say, at the same time as Simon asks, 'Would they keep the scenery?'

The twin who collects Elves looks pained and waves his hands in front of him. 'No, guys. It's a bar. They're just saying they'll put in a couple of larger tables in the corner so people can play there. If they want.'

Simon looks unimpressed. 'What so we're playing in the corner and the rest of the room is hipsters drinking fracking IPAs?'

'Yeah.' The twin sighs. He is our leader and I think he feels responsible for all of us.

Simon snorts. No one says anything after that. We put out a few trees, a farmhouse, a lake and two hills and start deploying our armies. We are nearly ready when Jonathan arrives.

'Ye gods man!' He says when he hears the club is closing. But when the twin tells him about the agreement with the bar downstairs, he looks relieved. 'So we'll play there then?'

The twin who collects Elves shrugs. 'Well I've got the baby due in June. So I probably won't be able to come for a bit.'

Dave laughs. He is the only one who does not seem to be taking this badly. 'You'll not sleep for a year mate! I'm telling you. Take it from me. Then you'll have another one and won't sleep for another year.' He laughs for a long time at his own joke.

'But really guys, you should go to the bar.' The twin who collects Elves looks around. I can see in his eyes he knows there is no way any of us are going.

We begin playing but we are quieter than usual. The only sounds are the patter of dice on the felt tables and the quiet murmur of conversation. Sometimes we hear nervous laughter from the smartly dressed men playing the Napoleonic wargame or muted exclamations from the Japanese students playing Magic the Gathering. We forget for a while that the club is closing. We forget about the bar downstairs, the world outside. Only occasionally, when the hobby painters go out to smoke on the balcony and the doors open and close, we hear a burst of shrieking laughter and the pulse of the sound system rising up from the canalside terrace. We hunch under the yellow lamps hanging low over the tables. We are as meek and quiet as the English monks of Lindisfarne and the low throb of bass from below is the sound of Viking oars beating ever closer over the water.

THE OTHER GAME

Before I played the Game I played the Other Game. We all did. The Other Game started in the seventies and grew from there. By the time I started playing when I was 13 it was on its sixth edition and was the biggest historical fantasy tabletop wargame in the world. But it had its problems.

Every year the company that ran the Other Game would revise the rules and release new, expensive miniatures with overpowered stats. So the miniatures you had were no longer any good and the new miniatures were essential if you wanted to win. We resented the price increases and the need to buy new miniatures but more than that we resented being treated as if we were stupid. It seemed to us that the company was only interested in profit and not in nurturing the community that existed around the Other Game at all. A lot of this anger had built up before I started playing and was something I adopted on behalf of the community, something I subscribed to, like a membership fee.

When I went to university there was a group of us who ran a games night every Thursday. We complained the Other Game was broken, the rules convoluted and warped, but we played anyway. It was still the only game running national tournaments where you could play with large rectangular blocks of miniatures, a hundred or so on each side, which is what you need to imagine you are the Field Marshal of an army.

In 2015 the company closed the Other Game, announcing that it was no longer profitable, the barrier to entry was too high and anyway, they wanted to put more resources into the new computer and online gaming market. I had moved to London by then. It was my first time living in a city and it seemed to me as dirty, crooked and dangerous as Ankh-Morpork. The flat I lived in with my ex-girlfriend was small and there was not much storage space so I sold most of my miniatures. No one I knew was playing the Other Game anyway. But I followed the whole thing closely online, the way you pay attention if you ever see your home town in the news.

So I read all about what happened when the company relaunched the Other Game the following year with new, simplified rules. The new version of the Other Game was designed to be played with only ten or so miniatures, positioned individually on round bases. It did not go down well on the community forums or the Reddit threads. The simplified rules were for children, people complained. And armies of ten or fifteen miniatures were a joke. That made us a Lance Corporal, Corporal at best. What were we supposed to do with our legions of Elves or Dwarves, with the thousands of pounds and hours we had invested? For some reason though it was the round bases that were the last straw. The Other Game was universally declared unplayable.

About the same time, two of the original designers from the Other Game quit the company and launched a Kickstarter, promising an entirely new game that would be a return to when the Other Game was good. The developers promised large blocks of infantry and, most importantly, square bases. They would produce miniatures, they said, but if you wanted to buy yours from another company or use your miniatures from the Other Game, that was okay. It was open source. The most important thing, they said, was the community. We had found a home again.

This is how the Game was born. I have been playing it at the club for five years now. Sometimes I do not talk to people from when I leave work on Friday to when I go to the club on Sunday. It is not that I am lonely. But sometimes I feel my aloneness like something heavy that is around me and also on me. It is on my back, like when you throw a blanket on your cat. You can tell she does not like it but for the most part she pretends to ignore it, only occasionally trying to twitch it off.

Ever since we talked about the club closing, the twin who collects Elves has been thinking of ways to get our gaming group name written down somewhere. The following week he suggested running a mini league among the seven of us and having a prize etched with the group name. But the week after that he dismissed the idea because then only one person would end up with the name. Another time he suggested a bench plaque, but Dave said that made it sound as if we were all dead and so that was thrown out too. In any case we do not even have a name though the twin who collects Elves said that could be worked out later.

This week he is visibly excited. He insists on buying us all a drink even though it is not his round. When he comes back and everyone has taken their drink from the tray he gathers us round the table. Dave wants to fetch the scenery and get on with it because he has to pick his boy up from football at four and Bryce says he needs to piss but the twin who collects Elves says it will be quick.

'You know how the club's closing in June and even if you do play – somewhere else – I won't be able to come for a bit?' He scratches the back of his head. It is something he does when he is thinking about taking a risk, like charging a pike block with his Elven Steeds or flying his Great Eagles into range of a gunline.

'I was thinking we should go out with a bang. I was thinking. We should enter the National Masters Tournament.' He paused, then goes on quickly. 'It's two weeks after the club closes. It's perfect – it will take our mind off it.'

Simon shrugs. 'I was going to enter that anyway.'

'No,' the twin says. 'All of us, together.'

Jonathan points at me. 'What even me and Robin?' We are the two worst players in the group.

The twin who collects Elves nods enthusiastically, but Simon does not look impressed. 'You all gonna' get owned.' He looks at me and Jonathan.

Simon is always taking his Daemons to tournaments. I hate playing him before a tournament because he is so competitive that it is impossible to immerse yourself in the world of the Game. Still, the week after the tournament I am keen to hear how he did. None of the rest of us have been to a tournament except Dave, and that was for the Other Game he says, many lifetimes ago. Simon is like our champion who we send out of the gates to fight on our behalf while we watch anxiously from the ramparts.

'We'll drive down in two cars. It will be like a road trip,' the twin who collects Elves is saying. He punches his fist into his palm. 'We'll be a real team you know. The more experienced gamers can help the rest of us. That's what a club is all about anyway.'

'Fuck it,' Bryce says. 'Yeah sounds sick.'

Simon looks from Jonathan to me. 'Guess we can write your lists for you at least.'

Then it is only Dave who is holding out, saying he can't take a whole weekend off from the boys but we all start persuading him and finally the twin who collects Elves points out that he is one of the two drivers and so actually it is critical that he comes and at that Dave relents and says, 'All right if it means you lads get down there, count me in.'

Jonathan raises his glass and shouts in a deep voice, 'The last march of the ents! Bururum!'

The bearded men playing Dungeons and Dragons look over in alarm. We hiss at Jonathan to shut up and the twin who collects Undead calls him a freak, but we are laughing and when we raise our glasses I really can feel the hairs standing up on the back of my neck.

From that point on all we can talk about is the tournament. Which armies should we bring? What kind of list should we take? But the first thing to decide on was our name. Simon suggests Death Squad but most of us think that is a bit heavy. Jonathan has lots of ideas. One of them is the Fangs of Fangorn, which I think is quite good, but the twin who collects Undead says not everyone is into that gay Lord of the Rings shit. Then the twin who collects Elves says how about Riddlers of Steel, like from Conan the Barbarian. No one hates it and since no one had a better idea it is decided.

I have always wanted to go to a tournament. When I was fourteen, I would read about them in the monthly magazine published by the company that ran the Other Game. I remember the glossy half page images of men holding tape measures standing behind immaculately painted armies. It was freeing to think that this was a way to grow up, that it was okay to live like this.

But ever since I bought my ticket to the National Masters Tournament it has only made me anxious. Each time I try to imagine what it will be like I can only see my opponent's hand calmly sliding his cavalry into the flank of my Halfling Spearlings and several dice rolls later, my own hands lifting them awkwardly off the table, the bright yellows and reds of my Halflings' jackets disappearing into the graveyard of my miniature case. Even thinking about it makes my hands pulse with frustration as if it is something liquid running through me. Of course I would do nothing, there at the table, and I do nothing, now, thinking about it, so the anger does what it always does. It slows and thickens and clots until it is no more than a small, heavy, cold thing in my chest that slips bit by bit like a movie extra falling through floors of scaffolding to land in the pit of my stomach.

Yes, there is no doubt about it. I will lose every game and embarrass myself and the rest of the group by association. I will bring dishonour on the Riddlers of Steel. Bilbo was right when he said it was a dangerous business going out your door. You step onto the road, and if you don't keep your feet, there's no knowing where you might be swept off to.

Most of the books I read are really the same book. The names and scenery changes but the story is the same. They are all about a young boy or girl who is a complete nobody and no good at anything. Until one day in a moment of high stress, they discover a secret power inside of them. The secret power might be that they can perform magic or are the rightful heir to the throne.

The world of the book might be home to dragons, elves or goblins, but the human elements are always from the Middle Ages. There are taverns, tankards and trebuchets and all the women are buxom and wear their hair in tresses. The forces of law and order are feudal and corrupt, so the cities are rife with crime and the land between city states is lawless and savage.

In these books the hero, who is always good, sets out on a long and arduous quest that takes him into these lawless places. They survive by their power alone, overcoming small time magicians or corrupt barons and bandits like mid-level bosses in a game. Until finally they confront the last boss, some false king or warlock who is the source of all the world's evil, and they defeat it.

THE HALFLING

It is a long, late winter and it gets harder and harder to wake up with the alarm clock. In the mornings, I lie in bed staring at the ceiling with its seventies popcorn plaster, blinking and listening to my housemates going to work. I scroll through the Game's various community forums, fending off pop-up ads. The air in my room is stale and my body leaden. I know I should clean but I do not. There are many things I should do but I do not do them. My things surround the bed. In the gloom they seem to twist out of the floor like the roots of the trees of Mirkwood: a clothes horse, a nest of computer cables, a dead laptop I might try to reprogram one day, pizza takeaway boxes, plates stacked unevenly over cutlery, crusted with dried pesto.

In the evenings, I watch cartoons, box sets, old Sci-Fi movie reruns. I read a little. I am like the pale, soft-skinned creatures in the Time Machine or the soft, jelly-covered anthropoids bred in pods in the Matrix. Sometimes I paint. I like to paint one miniature at a time. Each miniature might need seven colours: skin tone, hair, jacket, trousers, leather belt and boots, and metal blades with wooden handles. For every colour, I paint five layers: a base colour, a darker wash to shadow the recesses, the base colour again and then two layers of highlight. Gamers like Simon and Bryce paint their miniatures in batches of ten or twenty with three colours and two layers but they are only interested in doing the minimum. The way I do it takes a lot longer. I stay up into the small hours of the morning, painting under my five thousand Kelvin daylight bulb. I push back going to sleep, because to go to sleep is to wake up and to wake up is to go to work.

Winter drags into spring and preparations for the Tournament continue. Every week the twin who collects Elves gathers us together to go through the tactics of the Game. 'We could all learn something,' he says. But I know he means only me and Jonathan.

None of these training sessions go particularly well. One week Simon tells us we should be making spam lists. A spam list is a list with lots of one unit. For example, Simon always takes spam lists with lots of flying monsters. Most people play with one flying monster, but Simon takes at least three: a Sorceress on Manticore, a Witch Queen on Giant Harpy and a Daemon Prince on Dragon. The rest of his Daemon army is made up of succubi and the enslaved elven women who serve them. The elves are mostly naked and he paints their nipples and areola with a size one brush. He is the youngest of us and lives with his mother in Chingford.

Spam lists are considered unsportsmanlike because a balanced list will almost certainly lose to a spam list. The problem with spam lists though is if the other player also takes a spam list. Then the Game is effectively reduced to a round of Rock Paper Scissors. A spam list with lots of war machines will lose to a spam list with lots of flying monsters which will lose to a spam list with lots of cavalry which will lose to a spam list with lots of infantry which will lose to a spam list with lots of war machines.

When I ask Simon about this he shrugs and says winning a quarter of the time should be an improvement for me. He seems about to say more, but Jonathan says that a spam list sounds mighty boring to paint. Simon gets annoyed and says it is our funeral and the lesson ends there.

Another week Bryce tries to explain to us about manoeuvres. He has several empty MDF bases which he moves about the table to illustrate what he calls a peel charge. 'You have enemy units here and your units facing them here. It's a standoff, right. But if you move your shitty chaff unit right in their faces, you can bring your heavier units close in behind it. So next turn your chaff peels out the way and your heavy units charge in.'

'The hussars used to do something similar.' Dave is leaning on the table with his fists. 'They rode in two ranks, the first would shoot and move aside and the second rank would unleash another volley.'

Jonathan has not been paying attention but when Dave mentions the hussars he perks up and the two of them get into an animated conversation about the origin and purpose of the large wings of feathers the hussars wore on their back and so the lesson gets derailed.

This week it is the twin who collects Undead. He does not have a lesson as such but he produces some books from his bag and throws them on the table. He is hungover and all his movements are irritable. One is by Sun Tzu, one by Machiavelli and one by Nietzsche, which the twin who collects Undead says is actually not that relevant but is still good.

It is a bright spring day and the others are out on the club balcony. The twin looks outside and then back at us. The books lie on the table between us.

'There's no point in coming if you don't have a reasonable chance of winning a game.'

I glance at Jonathan, but he makes no move to touch the books so I scoop them up. Still, I am not sure what to say. 'Sure,' I say. 'That makes sense.'

The twin taps a cigarette against his knuckle. It is obvious he wants to go outside with the others. 'That's how tournaments work. Otherwise you're just dead weight. Worse, because you give an unfair advantage to anyone lucky enough to play you.'

'Okay.' I could not be holding the books any closer to my chest. Short of reading them right there in front of him, I do not know what he wants me to do.

When the twin who collects Undead has gone, Jonathan whistles. 'People are taking this tournament business very gravely.'

I feel a flash of annoyance at him. I am always being grouped with Jonathan at the bottom of the pile. But I wish I was not. I do not even need to be in the top tier with Simon and Bryce. The middle tier with Dave and the twins would be fine. Or maybe a new tier on my own below the middle tier but above Jonathan who sometimes I think is not even trying to win, or not even aware he is supposed to be trying to win.

I go to the toilet to be alone. The club toilet is out of order so I have to go downstairs to use the one in the hipster bar. I am about to urinate when a man swaggers into the toilet and stands at the next urinal, rocking on his heels, his shoulders thrown back manfully and his bald head glistening under the white light. I cannot urinate. There is nothing coming. I hear a humming noise, faint at first and then louder and then it is the only thing I can hear and somehow that humming noise is also the sound of my inability to urinate. I zip up and move away and lock myself in a cubicle. It is a flimsy lock, the sort that might easily be broken by a man I think. I can hear the jet of the man's piss cascading across the urinal. I wait for him to leave. I have to listen carefully because the sound of the doors might be someone else coming in and not him leaving. Though of course even if he did leave I still would not be safe because he will most likely be sitting somewhere in the bar with his friends when I come out of the toilet and I will have to put on a convincing performance of someone who had a good reason to rush so abruptly into a cubicle, yes perhaps dabbing a tissue at my nose as if that was what I had needed, or holding my side as if I had some kind of stomach bug, or some other skit, something to put out there that I had a good reason for hiding in the toilet cubicle, a reason that was nothing to do with a lack of manliness.

After I get out of the toilet and make it back to the club and we play and I lose and we pack up and I go home and make myself pasta and shower and climb into bed, I open the Game rulebook and stare at the page on Halflings for a long time. Halflings are rubbish, I think. They are slower and weaker than any other race. Why had I chosen them in the first place?

I was living with my parents when the Game launched. It was about the time my Ex-Girlfriend and I split up and I went back to live with them for a while. They put me in my brother's old room, because my room was being used for storage, my mother's quilting materials, mainly. It was strange being home again, at once comforting and demoralising. I was not sure if I had suffered a setback or whether I was rebooting to a truer version of myself.

When I was thirteen and played the Other Game I had collected Elves but when I came to choosing an army for the Game I chose Halflings, which are like hobbits from the Lord of the Rings. I knew from the stats they were not competitive but it seemed right. It still does. I live a small, regular life. There is my house, my work, the club. Sometimes I go for a drink at the Rose and Crown. The less I do the less I want to do and the more I am scared of doing it. So I am left to do as well as I can in the limited space in which my life is lived. On a bad day it seems that my ambitions have shrunk, quite literally, from Elf to Halfling but on a good day I think instead that my honesty has grown.

I pick up one of the books from the twin who collects Undead and start flicking through it. It is Sun Tzu, the Art of War. Sun Tzu says that if you know the enemy and know yourself you need not fear the result of a hundred battles.

That makes sense. If you know everything about everyone of course you will come out on top. Then Sun Tzu says, if you know yourself but not the enemy, for every victory gained you will also suffer a defeat. This seems like a more realistic goal. I never know what enemy I will face. Even though I know which army everyone plays at the club, I do not know what lists they will bring each week. And at the tournament, I do not know which armies I will be facing. I read the line again. Sun Tzu is saying I can get a fifty per cent win rate if I know myself. That seems manageable. I turn back to the page on Halflings in the rulebook. I am thinking about Sun Tzu and about that fact that Halflings are slow and weak, but also cheap, when I get the idea. The idea to make a Haffling infantry spam list.

THE PRECIOUS

I make an immediate start on my infantry spam list. There is no time to lose. It is six weeks until the tournament and only four weeks until our last game at the club. I order six boxes of plastic Halfling Spearlings. Each box contains eight sprues and each sprue contains the parts to make five Halflings: legs, torsos, arms holding various weapons and an assortment of heads. It takes a long time to clip the parts from the sprues and superglue them together but in the end it is done and I have two hundred and forty Halfling Spearlings, some thrusting their spears forward, some carrying them over their shoulders as they march and others leaning on them wearily.

Because there is such a large amount of Halflings and such a small amount of time, there is no question of painting them one by one as I usually do. So I decide to do what the Gamers do. I will batch paint all two hundred and forty Halflings at the same time.

This raises a problem. For usually I Blu-Tack my Halflings onto corks, each of which I skewer onto a pin that is stuck up through a notice board on my painting desk. But even when I search in all the spare parts boxes under my bed I can only gather together sixty or so corks.

I get around this problem by sawing each of the corks into four roughly equal pieces, and adding more pins to the bottom of the noticeboard until I have a grid of twenty by twelve pins.

But this solution is not ideal. For as I work my way along

the first row of Halflings, painting their faces, hands and feet with the first layer of skin tone, I can see that as I reach the second, third and so on rows, it will take me longer and longer to pick up a Halfling. The quarter corks are so stubby and the pins packed so closely that it will be almost impossible for me to get my hand in far enough to pick up the quarter of cork.

Still, I keep on as well as I can, picking each Halfling up by the shaft of its spear though of course this is only a short-term solution for there is no way I can do that when I come to paint the spear shafts themselves.

The worst of it is that there is no way to spread the quarter of cork out more than they already are because of the limiting dimensions of the notice board. Of course if the quarters of corks were not in a grid of twenty by twelve but instead in a single long line then there would not be a problem because it would be easy to pick up each and every quarter of cork. But this would be completely impractical because even if every cork was spaced no more than a centimetre apart, the line would go on for nearly ten metres.

For a long time I am convinced there is no way to solve this problem beyond some kind of circular conveyor belt and sometimes as I paint I think I might as well abandon entirely the idea of batch painting them all in time for the tournament.

Lying in bed in the small hours of the morning turning and turning the problem over in my head it occurs to me that there might be a simple and elegant solution to the problem. Yes, it strikes me that instead of trying to space the pins farther apart, I should actually be spacing them closer together, which is to say I should have twice as many pins arranged, not twenty by twelve, but twenty by twenty four, with the quarters of cork skewered to the twelve nearest rows. They would be pressed so close together as to be touching but that did not matter for when I finished with a Halfling from the first row I would replace its quarter of cork – not on a pin from its original row – but on the nearest available row at the back, and the quarters of cork from the second row the same, and so on. In this way the quarters of cork with the next row of Halflings to be painted would always be at the front and it would be the easiest thing in the world to pick them up and paint them without touching the spear shaft or any other part of the model. Once a layer of painting was completed and all the quarters of cork were skewered on the back twelve rows of pins, I would simply turn the board around and follow exactly the same procedure in reverse.

'Holy fuck!' Simon says when I open my miniature case.

My Halfling Spearlings do look impressive. It is one thing to see them at home on my painting desk, but it is quite another to see them deployed in long ranks across the tabletop. They stretch right across my deployment zone. Everyone is asking me what my plan is and how I painted them so quickly. I explain about Sun Tzu and the quarters of corks and the pins and how once I had a system down I was able to do it in two weeks. Simon is biting his cuticles and looking nervously at his own army list and the twin who collects Undead slaps me on the back and says I am onto something. Later, one of the smartly dressed men who play the Napoleonic wargame saunters over and peers over his glasses at my Halfling Spearlings and gives me a small nod of approval before wandering away. It is a good day.

I always lose against Simon but this time I win because every time he takes out a company of Halfling Spearlings there are two more to take their place and at one point I even manage to surround his Daemon Prince on Dragon with sixty Halfling Spearlings and kill it although many Halflings lose their lives in the encounter.

When he has finished packing up, Simon mutters something about dumb motherfucking infantry spam lists and strides off to the far side of the room. He spends the next hour with the teenagers who play cyberpunk skirmish games and leaves without saying goodbye to us. I think in Simon's head, the only unsportsmanlike list is an infantry spam list because that is the one list he struggles most to win against.

Jonathan and me take the train part of the way home together. The sun made points of light on the car windscreens. I feel briefly warm towards all strangers. These are the local townsfolk, I think. Little do they know that a great battle has been fought in the converted warehouse on the industrial estate. Never have so many owed so much to so small a few.

Jonathan is talking but I am not listening. I am always a little embarrassed taking the train with him. He talks loudly and does not seem to care what people think of him.

'It's an alloy man!' He has been trying to find a word to describe nerd culture. 'You have all these elements – the pantheistic occultism of the sixties, the campness of the seventies, the comic culture of the eighties and then in the nineties you've got superhero graphic novel culture. It's a potent alloy. Greater than the sum of its parts.'

He stares out the window and licks his teeth. The warehouses and car parks are replaced by rows of narrow terraced houses and, rising behind them, the pillars of tower blocks. He sways as the train picks up speed. He is holding the rubber handgrip over his head with both hands and his miniature case is wedged between his feet.

'And no one was interested. For decades! It was our thing.'

Jonathan is not much older than me. I supposed he means we, nerds.

'Then Lord of the Rings happened. And Star Wars. And don't even talk to me about Harry Potter. Now every movie is either fantasy historical or superhero.'

'Isn't that a good thing?' I am feeling magnanimous.

I remember when I was eleven my mother bought two tickets to the opening night of The Fellowship of the Ring. Before the movie started she nudged me and pointed. A few rows in front was a man in a wizard's hat. I did not reply because I was submerged in a state of deep concentration. It was not until the hobbits made it over the Ford of Bruinen that I realised I was gripping the sides of the seat so tightly that the tendons all the way along my forearms were stinging with pain. It was not only the movie that I loved. It was the fact that so many other people, even my mother, were sharing in this world.

'But they change it!' The train stops and Jonathan takes the opportunity to sweep the hair off his face and pinch at his nose. 'Like that plotline with Arwen and Aragorn. Tolkien was a frigid Catholic for Pete's sake!'

I bite my lip and try to concentrate on what Jonathan is saying. It is not easy. People are looking at us. I remember when we got home after the movie I overheard my parents joking about the man in the wizard's hat. I heard the clink of wine glasses and their laughter from the bathroom where I was brushing my teeth and was embarrassed.

'They took this precious alloy and melted it down and mixed it with their lowest common denominator metals and they give it back to us with the arrogance of a gift-giver. A gift-giver I tell you!'

Jonathan likes making compound words. He reads a lot of Old Norse and Anglo-Saxon: Beowulf, Prophecy of the Völva, that kind of stuff. He can even speak a few lines of Old English, which he imagines is how Dwarves speak in the Game. He says it is more Tolkien than Tolkien.

The train rattles through a tunnel. In the gloom, Jonathan leans in close and hisses, 'The precious! They stole it from us!'

The train leaves the tunnel and the carriage bursts with light again. Everyone is staring at us now.

Jonathan laughs loudly at his own impression. He is one of those people who is funny but not for the reasons he thinks he is funny.

'Aha this is me!' Jonathan says as the train pulls into the station. He picks up his miniature case and grips my shoulder with one hand, which is how Elves greet and say goodbye to each other. I tap his shoulder in return.

The train waits at the station to help regulate the service. I watch Jonathan join the press of people shuffling slowly over the footbridge. He holds his miniature case close to his chest and takes small steps, his head twitching up and down as he tries to note the position of other people's feet. He seems smaller and less certain from this distance.

I get off the train and walk the few streets to my house. Midway along there's a bridge over the railway and the wall is backed by a steel fence topped with barbed wire. When I turn onto my road, it seems as if the air thickens. It is something heavy that is around me and also on me. In Year Seven I played Magic the Gathering on my lunch breaks. I played with three friends on the picnic tables along the edge of the playground and no one paid us any attention. Until one summer, everyone wanted to play. The picnic tables were so busy that sometimes we had to play on the floor. Even Ben Burton who was the class clown and well loved, asked us to sit with him one time to teach him how to play. He cleared his friends off the picnic table and beckoned us to join him from where we sat cross-legged on the floor. He was holding a new deck his mum had bought him that weekend, still in its shrink wrap. But in autumn, every single person who started playing that summer stopped. It was only the four of us again and no one sat with us at the picnic tables or paid us any attention. So no, I do not trust them with our worlds I thought. I do not trust people like Ben Burton who offered me a seat at my own picnic table and who probably does not even remember trading Mesa Pegasus with me on lunch break in 1997.

THE META

It is not easy to push through the smoking area to get to
the stairs. Today is the last day of the club before the whole
warehouse is shut for redevelopment. The hipster bar
downstairs is having a closing party and on top of that, it is
the first hot day of summer.

I have never liked the summer. The heat, the sweat, the sun
cream, the way my clothes and hair stick to my skin. I should
be indoors where it is cool. The heat forces me into shorts,
t-shirts and flip-flops. I must consider my skin and my body
which are pale and scrawny, respectively. I am embarrassed
about my toes, which are odd sizes. But everyone else seems
to love it. They shed their clothes as if they had never wanted
to wear them in the first place. The streets are full of flesh,
midriff and thigh, chest, breast and bicep.

The men wear their shirts open to the nipple as if their
hair has forced the shirt apart and the women wear low cut
tops and shorts shorter than their pockets. It is hard not to
look at them but I know I must not look at them because I
know they do not want to be looked at but I do not understand
why they wear so little that covers so little if they do not want
to be looked at and it is hard and it makes me confused and
frustrated though of course I see they probably do – actually
– yes, they do want to be looked at, a certain way, sometimes,
by some people, but it is not me, no it is not me that they want
to look at them.

I am not so good around women. I saw a beautiful woman one Tuesday at the Rose and Crown. She was sitting at the bar with a man, she leaning forward and laughing at something he had said, and he leaning back, smirking and running his hand through his hair. For days after I went over and over that image and the more I did, the more ungrateful and self-satisfied and smug he seemed, the more of a Casanova I imagined him to be and so the more violated I felt on her behalf, that she should be treated so frivolously, so lightly, so philanderingly, when in fact not even the smallest part of him, not even one of the hairs on his head, not one of the long, dark, voluminous hairs on his head that he was always running his big hand through so manfully, sweeping them off his forehead and not afraid at all of exposing his hairline which was of course not receding, no, not even one of those hairs were worthy of her.

I went back to the Rose and Crown the following Tuesday in the hope she would be there but she was not. What was I hoping for anyway? That I, some pale, gelatinous deep sea creature, might emerge from behind a pillar, stammering, 'Hullo? Um. Hullo?'

I am not like the twin who collects Undead. The twin who collects Undead is always talking about his sexual exploits. That is what Dave calls them. As soon as the twin starts talking, Dave laughs loudly and says, 'Oh boy, another episode of sexual exploits!' I think Dave enjoys them more than anyone else. The stories always end with the twin who collects Undead either having or not having sex with someone.

It is a relief to make the cool of the stairwell and to close the heavy double doors of the club behind me. The club is having a closing party. The owner has hung a banner over the bar painted with the slogan, 'Not with a bang but with a whimper.' The last four letters have been crossed out and above them is written, 'skey'. It is a whiskey night.

Everyone is drinking. The two grey haired hobby painters are already quite drunk and one of them is reminiscing loudly about the time his Wood Elf army was featured in the magazine published by the company that ran the Other Game. Even the two Napoleonic players who usually only drink fruit juice are sipping shandies.

As soon as I near our table, Simon comes up to me. He is keen to tell me he has changed his army following his defeat the week before and I will not be beating him again. He has substituted his Witch Queen on Giant Harpy for several Bolt Throwers. 'To take out your infantry,' he says. The twin who collects Elves starts pairing people off randomly but Simon insists on playing me. 'If I can crack an infantry spam list,' he says, 'I've cracked the Spanish meta.'

Simon is always talking about the meta. The meta is the way the Game is played by a group. Anticipating and outwitting the Game's meta is a game in itself. Our local meta is dictated by Simon and Bryce who play Daemons and Orcs, both of which are fast moving, aggressive combat armies. So any army we bring to the club has to be able to deal with that.

But though Simon and Bryce are powerful at a local meta,

they are not powerful at a global meta. Simon says the UK meta is cavalry armies. Though you never know, he says, because in one tournament just before Christmas, a group of Spanish players turned up and destroyed everyone. It caused quite a stir. After, the Spanish players posted pictures of themselves arriving at Madrid-Barajas Airport, joking around in the bright sun, their trophies in the crook of their arms. One of them even knelt on the floor and kissed the tarmac like a homecoming conquistador. All of that was because the Spanish meta is dominated by Goblin armies and lists with vast numbers of cheap infantry and the UK armies with their tight bands of cavalry did not have an answer to that.

It is a long game and ends in a draw. It would have been boring if Simon had not given a running commentary about the tactical implications of every move. I nodded along wisely but most of it went over my head. Still, he has never talked to me about tactics before and I feel that now I have my new infantry spam list, for the first time he respects me. When the games are over, we sit around drinking whiskey and arguing about Star Wars. Or rather, we argue about toxic masculinity in Star Wars. Or rather, we argue about whether it is true that Poe is a symbol of toxic masculinity in Star Wars Episode XIII.

The twin who collects Elves read an article a few days ago about how Poe's decision to commit the final few rebel forces to a botched attack against the advice of General Leah was a conscious move by the screen writers designed to make Poe seem rash and impulsive and serve as an example of toxic masculinity.

Dave says he himself cannot keep up with all the lingo like toxic masculinity.

The twin who collects Undead has not read the article but he says, 'Was he rash, was he fuck! He did the right thing and he's getting framed. Feminist agenda. End of.'

Simon hides his mouth with his hand as he laughs. 'Right on man.'

Bryce stares into his whiskey glass and swirls it gently.

The twin who collects Undead is always saying he hates feminists and Simon is always agreeing with him. It comes up more often than you would think. I do not know about the twin, but I do not think Simon actually knows what a feminist is. I think what Simon hates is the suggestion he is powerful when he does not think of himself as powerful at all. Maybe he is powerful at a global meta, but really he is so shy and small that he is not powerful at a local meta.

'Attack is the best form of defence,' the twin who collects Undead concludes.

'Codswallop!' says Jonathan, who always plays too defensively.

Up until now the argument has been somewhat stilted, as if we are actors who have not rehearsed their lines, but now it gathers speed.

Bryce looks up from his whiskey. 'Poe got a lot of useful pilots killed bro.'

The argument moves seamlessly into contesting the exact number of remaining rebel forces at the time of the attack, their battle readiness, how long it takes to train new recruits and the minimum necessary rest time needed for front line troops, all of which is what we like arguing about most anyway.

When I leave the sky is heavy with Sunday evening dread. The beer garden downstairs is heaving with bodies squeezed up against the sound system set up by the canal. I keep my head down and push through to the street. Cranes spread like nets over the rooftops. All the warehouses round here are coming down. As I get closer to the station I pass the new developments. Only a scattering of flats have been sold and yellow light spills from them onto the balconies, illuminating the splayed fronds of plants, Brompton bikes, fold-up bistro tables and chairs.

People are still streaming out of the train station. You would think there was a music festival or football match or political rally. But they are here for the bars that brew their own beer and coffee shops that roast their own coffee. It is because of them the club is closing. In a roundabout way, it is because of them. Certainly it is not because of us. It is not because of us that the area is becoming more popular, that whole grids of streets are being turned into new build flats and now even the club, the warehouse, the whole street is being knocked down for redevelopment. Even if it is not them who are buying the flats in the new developments, it is because the people buying the flats want to be close to them, or want to go to the same bars as them, or want to say they live near the bars where they go. In any case, it is because of them, in a roundabout way, the club is closing.

Everyone knows the best articles on the Game's tactics are on Briohmarblog. I have read them all before but I decide to read them once more. It is Friday evening, the night before the tournament and I want it to be tomorrow already.

My miniature case has been packed for hours. I have checked and rechecked all my units. After our game Simon suggested I drop two of my Halfling Spearling companies and reinstate my Pony Riders to give me some fast moving chaff. So my list is now: three Spearling legions and four smaller Spearlings companies, two bands of Pony Riders, three Ballista, one company of Hippogriff knights, a Magician and my Cockagriff. A Cockagriff is a magical creature with the body, tail, and back legs of a lion and the head and wings of a rooster. I am worried its wings will snap on the journey so I have packed emergency superglue and Blu-Tac. I also have two sandwich bags of dice, two measuring tapes, my laser pen, the Game rule book, the Game extension rule book, ten printed copies of my army list and a tray to carry my miniatures between games.

I have laid out my outfit for tomorrow which I only do for big days, like if I have an appraisal at work. My clothes are folded on my chair, from top to bottom in the order I put them on. In the perfect world I would own one set of clothes. Every night I would wash it in the sink with a bar of soap. It would dry overnight and every morning I would wear it again. All else is vanity.

I make myself a cup of tea, turn a fresh page in my notepad and open up Briohmarblog. By way of introduction,

Briohmar says he has been playing tabletop wargames for twenty years. Before the Game he played the Other Game and before that, other games I have never heard of. He is a retired US military intelligence analyst who was assigned to a unit that taught MDMP (Military Decision Making Process). His articles are structured around the nine principles of war: MOOSEMUS (Mass, Objective, Offensive, Security, Economy of Force, Manoeuvre, Unity of Command, Simplicity and Surprise). Some of these principles do not seem that relevant to the Game, but the acronyms are impressive and I write them down.

In his first article, Briohmar divides the Game's units into categories like anvils, hammers and chaff. Anvils are units which can take a hit and hold, hammers are units which do the hitting, and chaff are cheap, expendable units. Briohmar says a good general must be prepared to let his chaff units die and he quotes Gunnery Sergeant R. Lee Ermey in Full Metal Jacket who says, 'Marines die. That's what they're there for, but the Marine Corps lives forever and so you live forever.'

I love rousing speeches in movies. Like in The Return of the King when King Theoden rides along the crest of the hill, running his sword against the spears of the Rohirrim shouting, 'Arise riders of Theoden! A sword day, a red day and the sun rises!' Or in Henry V when Laurence Olivier addresses his men, rousing them for one final assault. His voice leaps louder as the camera pans out and he shouts, 'The game's afoot - follow your spirit, and upon this charge cry, God for Harry! England, and Saint George!' His horse rears up and he pulls it round and gallops out of the gully and all the soldiers charge after him shouting, 'God for Harry! England and Saint George!'

Maybe I love these speeches because I want to be a hero. Or maybe these scenes allow everyone to be a hero. I do not need to be Theoden or Henry V. It is enough to be a Rider of Rohan or an English longbow man, to be myself, or a version of myself with all worry erased. They relieve me of my feelings of uselessness and anxiety about what I am supposed to do with my life and relieve me of my responsibility for those feelings as well. They make everything simple. All I have to do is follow.

It takes me a long time to get to sleep. There is a line in this Nietzsche book I am reading that I keep turning over in my head. It goes, 'I have always laughed at the weaklings who think themselves good because their claws are blunt.' It makes me feel small and trapped that line. I do not have an answer to it. I cannot refute or escape it. I try to think what Gandalf would say in response to it because often that helps me feel better about things people have said to me. But it does not help this time.

THE TOURNAMENT

We drive down in two cars. Me and Jonathan are with the twins, and Simon and Bryce are in the other car with Dave. The twin who collects Undead is driving. It is early morning and the roads are empty as we pull onto the flyover going west out of London. The twins argue over the music. I stare out of the window as clumps of tower blocks give way to copses of trees.

Mist puddles low over the fields on either side of the car. I always think of the Romans in the countryside. I read a story once about a Roman legion which got lost in the mist and never returned. They went beyond where the straight roads stopped and they did not come back.

The venue is a long, low warehouse on an industrial estate down by the estuary. We clamber out the car to stretch our legs while we wait for Dave and the others. Another car pulls in as we are standing there. A bald man in a red t-shirt pushes himself out with difficulty, his miniature case clutched in the crook of his arm. He leans down to blow a kiss and the woman behind the wheel says something like, 'Good luck Dewie!' As he stands, he sees us looking at him and bobs his head before hurrying inside.

When Dave arrives, we take our miniatures out of the boot and cross the car park. On either side of the doors into the venue are two life size plastic statues: an Elf and a Dwarf. It is not until we pass between them that I realise how nervous I am. We are here. Part of me wants it to be over already and to be home and reading about it on one of the community blogs.

We bunch together inside the hall. It is bigger than I imagined. A strip of carpet runs all the way from our feet to the bar at the back of the hall and spreading out on either side of it are long rows of tables. Maybe ten rows of tables, long enough for five or more games on each side.

'Ye gods man,' Jonathan says.

I expect the twin who collects Elves to lead us but he stands still and blows air from his cheeks. It is the other twin who nods to the far corner with his chin.

We follow him towards a space at the end of the bar where a group of people are clustering round a large noticeboard pinned with papers, listing times and table numbers for the first game.

Once we have our table numbers we go back outside so the twin who collects Undead can smoke. More and more people are arriving, mostly men in black t-shirts with gothic logos printed on the front, some in chequered shirts and several thin men in long-sleeved t-shirts. A few people must recognise Simon from previous tournaments because they wave and shout things like, 'Good luck out there lads!' or, 'Break a leg boys!' Simon gives them a crooked thumbs up and says, 'Safe.'

At one point four men with dark beards, baseball caps and tattoos stride past. Simon waits for them to enter the hall before jerking his thumb behind him and hissing that they were the Spanish players. He is as excited as if they are celebrities. He starts talking about the tactical weaknesses of the Spanish meta but Bryce interrupts him. 'If any of us draws one of those guys, the only tactic is to hide in the fracking toilet.' This makes everyone laugh, even Simon. Maybe it is the adrenaline or the fact that we are all together or the way people recognise Simon but I start to feel okay about everything.

At nine forty five we go to our tables. I am on table 16 against a Dwarf player from the Bedfordshire Brawlers who is already there when I arrive. He is a big man with a messy beard who sits with his elbows on the table and his hands clasped together. He does not speak as I hang my jacket on my chair and begin to unpack my miniatures.

Most Dwarf armies are slow so the twin who collects Elves said my plan should be to send my Pony Riders and Cockagriff forward to kill his cannons and only then move forward with my mass of infantry. But as soon as I arrive at the table I realise this is not going to be an option. The Dwarf army is arranged on a small wooden tray and I can see it is the fastest Dwarf army it is possible to make.

Each Halfling Spearling unit I take from my case seems smaller and more vulnerable than the one before. I know I should be thinking of a new plan but I cannot. All I can think is, Fuckity fuck fuck on a loop without a break.

Briohmar says it is essential to arrange your units in formations so they can support each other. When he was in the 1st Armoured Division in Operation Desert Storm in early 1991, the M1 Abrams tanks always worked in pairs. The Iraqis tried to climb on top of the tanks to plant explosives in the hatches and the wingman's job was to hose off his partner by spraying the top of his tank with 7.62 mm machine gun fire. This was not enough to damage the tank, Briohmar says, but it sure did a number on the enemy infantryman standing on it.

We take it in turns to place units on the battlefield. I know I should be arranging them in formations and have a clear objective for each one like Briohmar says but my head is all in a mix and I do not have a plan for any of them. By the third turn most of my Spearlings are queued up in a long valley. The legion at the front is stuck in combat with a Dwarf Ironfist unit and the valley is too narrow for the others to come forward and support it so the whole advantage of my overwhelming numbers is lost. I imagine it is chaos in there. The units at the front trying to retreat and the ones at the back trying to advance. When his three companies of Dwarf Badger Riders crest the hill on the left side of the valley and I cannot turn to face them, I know it is the beginning of the end.

After we submit our result to the referee pacing between the tables, I go to get a coffee from the machine near the entrance. It is only while I am waiting for the coffee to pour that I realise how intense that Dwarf player was. After the obligatory exchange of compliments on each other's miniatures at the start of the game, he did not say much at all. It was sinister, the silent, methodical way he destroyed my units. I take a few deep breaths to steady myself. It is definitely more fun to read about tournaments in a magazine than to be at one. I thought everyone would be like our group, but of course that was stupid. They were just people who happened to play the Game.

I go back to the noticeboard to see where my next game is. I am on table 98 against a Silvan Creatures player. In theory the games should get easier now, I tell myself, as I drop down the ranking and play worse and worse players. Who knew, that Dwarf player might go on to win the whole tournament.

The Silvan Creatures player is a woman wearing a green hoodie with a print of a moon on the centre. When I turn up to the table she says, 'Hi, I'm the token woman.' Later she says, 'I must be the only woman who plays in the whole country.' And then, 'Only kidding, but seriously I'm the only one who's stupid enough to turn up to these things.'

Earlier I thought I saw a few women. But now the games have started I see they are not playing. They are standing at the bar. A few are chatting and others are swiping at their phones.

Her army is a rapid attack Silvan Creatures list with lots of centaurs, wolves, hawk riders and giant eagles. By turn three, my Halfling Spearlings are mostly boxed up in a small village at the centre of the board with her units surrounding me. Once again the advantage of my numbers has been lost. This was not the plan at all. Now all I can do is defend. Briohmar says that when he was an infantryman, his view on defence was: If they tell you to dig in, dig well. The hole you fight from is the hole you'll be buried in.

I sigh. We are surrounded, I think. We have marched beyond where the straight roads stop and we cannot go back. I imagine the shapes of the centaurs' flanks moving in and out of the early morning mist. We clench our spear shafts, peering into the trees. The company sergeant's voice carries through the village. Do not give up the wall! I hear the creak and clank of the ballistae as they are wheeled into position at the gate.

'You going to sit those Spearlings behind that wall for the whole game?'

I look up. 'Oh. Yeah, probably.'

She snorts. 'All right. I'll kill them last then.'

She has a habit of telling me what she is going to do before she does it. It is annoying because even though she tells me in advance, and I have time to do something about it, it still works. I have to get a grip. But it is too late for that. She wins on the fourth turn. After we have put our models back on our trays we still have more than half an hour.

She looks around the room and narrows her eyes. 'My last game, the guy was such a douche.' She pretends to gag. 'I don't know why some guys are like that.'

I nod, thinking of the silent Dwarf. 'My first game wasn't much fun.'

She picks at the plastic label round her Fanta bottle until it puckers and rips.

We are two lost souls, I think. Then I am annoyed at myself for being weird. But who knows, maybe later we would hook up.

She pushes her glasses up her nose. 'Anyway it was nice playing against you.'

'Yeah, same.' I stand and struggle into my jacket. Thing is

I don't want to be nice to play against. For once, I want to win.

The burger van is out of burgers by the time I get there so I buy a hot dog. I was hoping to find Simon or Bryce so I could ask them for tactical advice but I can only see Jonathan, sitting in the sun on the wall near Dave's car.

Jonathan raises his hand as I approach. 'How fares thee sir!'

I look around but no one pays him any attention. Everyone is hunched over their paper plates. I sit beside him on the wall. 'I'm not faring so well actually.'

Jonathan slaps me on the back. 'I lost both my games gloriously. In the first one, my army died to the dwarf. Would you believe! The bards are already calling it the Last Stand of Stonehaven!'

I tell him about the Dwarf player who had silently demolished me.

Jonathan nods. 'Even Dwarves can be cock wallopers.' He tells me his first opponent took such an objection to him referring to his units by their fictional names that he called over the referee. But the second person he played had been a real gentleman. He had the most beautiful woodland themed Elf army, painted in autumnal yellows and reds. Jonathan sighs as he remembers it.

We are silent as we finish our hot dogs. I check the time. It is five to two.

'We should probably go in.' I do not really want to. Because we have lost both our games we will be on the bottom thirty two tables.

Jonathan raises his fist in the air and makes a trumpet sound. 'For ruin and a red dawn! Forth Eorlingas!' We throw our paper plates in the recycling and go back into the hall.

My third game is on table 104 against Elves. The Elf player is a tall, thin man with a neat side parting. His miniatures are meticulously painted, his halberdiers in particular. He has layered their cloaks so finely that the deep wine-coloured shadow of each fold's recess gives way imperceptibly to a white highlight on the ridge of the crease. Facing up to them across the table, my Halfling Spearlings look like a Reception class project.

'Those cloaks look great,' I say.

He thanks me. He has a slow, measured voice. I watch him scan my army. Finally he says, 'The wood on your ballista is quite realistic.'

His phone rings and he answers it. While he is distracted, I take from my pocket the piece of paper on which I have drawn several diagrams showing the different deployment formations from Briohmar's article. I was too embarrassed to take it out earlier, but I study it now. I look at the terrain and his units and my units and then at the diagrams again. Yes, I think. This is my moment.

But it is not my moment. On my first turn when I have moved all my units, I say, 'I think that's the end of my movement phase.' It is more to make conversation than anything else. Then I see I have forgotten to move my Magician into the cover of some trees. 'Actually I just need to move this guy.'

The Elf player frowns. 'But you have ended your movement phase.'

I am already leaning over the table to measure the distance. I look up. 'But I haven't done any shooting yet.' At the club we play that a phase ends when you do the first action of the next phase.

He sucks air though his teeth as if this is a tough and regrettable moment for him too. 'You did declare it though.'

I straighten up from the table. He could not be serious. But he was.

I continue with my turn and tell myself it does not matter but sure enough, on his turn he shoots my Magician with his archers and kills him. My hands and arms are itching with anger. I squeeze and release the metal bars underneath the table and wait for it to pass but it does not pass. You should not care, I say to myself. It is only a stupid game. But another part of me is saying, but I do care! Not about the game but about this Elf man being such a dick. It is unfair. It is unfair that he is going to win because he is such a dick. It is unfair that people who are dicks are always winning everywhere at everything.

From that point on I am nervous and check and recheck everything before I declare the end of a phase and because of that I start running out of time on the clock and begin rushing and making mistakes and I remember Briohmar said Napoleon once told his generals that they could have more of any resource they wanted except one – time. About halfway through the game I mis-measure the charge distance of his Phoenix Riders and it turns out they are in range of my last Halfling Spearlings legion after all. On his turn, he charges them in the flank and kills them. When I have to remove them, I am sperging so much on the inside that my hands are trembling.

At the end we shake hands. I think he might at least say something by way of apology, but he only smiles in a way that is not really a smile at all. So to prompt him I say, 'I was pretty unlucky there eh?'

He looks at me as if he has only just seen me, even though we have been playing for ninety minutes, and says in that slow, measured voice, 'You made some bad decisions.' Then he starts placing his miniatures neatly back onto his tray.

It is times like these that the magic falls away, like a theatre backdrop cut from its rails and I realise I am not a Halfling Field Marshall rallying his troops on the village border to meet whatever force is gathering in the mist between the trees. I am a twenty seven year old man moving plastic miniatures around a table in a hall that smells like a school gym, and all those things that were briefly bright and clear and beautiful are murky and knotted and ugly again.

We have to go back to the boards to see who we are drawn against for our final game. I scan down the final tables looking for my name. When I find it, I let out an involuntary sigh. I am on table 123 and I am playing Jonathan.

I pick my way between the tables to the corner. I have dropped from table 16 to 98 to 104 and now I am on 123. There are only 128 tables at the tournament. Though I suppose that does mean there are ten players worse than us.

Jonathan throws his hands up when I approach. 'Wilcuman! Let the smallest of spear-shakers do battle!'

It is hard not to smile. I am unpacking my dice when I notice the rest of our row of tables is empty. Tables 124 to 128.

'Wait,' I jerk my thumb. 'Where are the other guys?'

'Oh they're empty.' Jonathan has put his Brewmaster in a watchtower and is now struggling to get him out again. 'The referee said there's always some drop outs. People are ill and stuff.'

I nod but cannot look at him. So we are literally the last table. Shit. Today has been a disaster. What is the point of beating Jonathan when we are from the same club? But I push the thought from my mind. I can either come last or second last. The only thing that matters now is winning this game.

Jonathan sets up his Dwarves in a defensive castle regardless of who he plays so I decide to deploy in an echelon formation. I think about what Bryce taught us about peel charges and I arrange my units on the left flank in such a way that the bands of Pony Riders in front could move sharply to the right, allowing my Hippogriff Knights to charge forward into his Shieldwall company. For two turns, this formation marches up the board until finally they are within striking distance. If he does not do something .in his turn I can execute my plan.

On his turn, he moves a few of his units but not his Shieldwall company. 'Right, that's all my movement done.' He reaches for the dice and starts humming and hawing about which of his cannons to shoot first. Then he says, 'Ah I didn't move my Relic.'

His Relic is a custom built miniature, with four dwarves in gold ceremonial armour carrying a curtained palanquin which Jonathan says contains the bones of some dead dwarf.

He starts to measure the distance.

I did not notice the Relic before but now I see he has left it out in the open, within charge range of my Cockagriff. If I can pull off the peel charge on the left and kill his Relic on the right I will probably win the game. 'You ended your movement phase,' I say.

He looks at me, not understanding then laughs. 'Come on!' When I do not speak he adds, 'We're talking about the Bones of the First Brewmaster of Stonehaven! It's totally unbelievable they wouldn't retreat to the safety of the trees.'

'You ended your movement phase,' I say again. 'It's a tournament.' I can hear my voice. I am trying to sound measured but I sound shrill.

'But you're going to kill it with your Rooster thingummy.'

'Cockagriff,' I say. And then, 'Yeah maybe.'

'I see.' Jonathan sighs as if I have grievously insulted him. He folds up his tape measure and places it on the table. His movements are slow and heavy. He is quiet for the rest of his turn and when he is done, he sits, rests his chin on his hands and says, 'Your turn, oath-breaker.'

I tut audibly. He is so melodramatic! I wish he would stop trying so hard to make me feel bad when if he was actually my friend he should be happy for me. I move through the turn quickly, executing the peel charge into his Shieldwall and charging my Cockagriff into his Relic. There is not much chit-chat. When it comes to rolling dice for combat I hurry through it. Usually we make a big deal over game-deciding dice rolls, sometimes even drumming our hands on the table, but it does not feel right this time. When I roll, Jonathan stands for the first time since the end of his turn and hunches over the table to scan the dice. Then he sinks back in his chair and says, 'So pass the last Dwarves of Stonehaven.'

Later we stand outside near the burger van which is still out of burgers waiting for the results to be announced. Everyone is drinking beers from plastic cups except Dave and the twin who collects Elves who are driving. We discuss our games and describe the successful manoeuvres we pulled off. Simon is bragging about getting a draw against one of the Spanish players. The twin who collects Elves is trying to calculate how many points we have won as a club.

'I played some real cock wallopers,' Jonathan says abruptly. He is staring at me.

The twin who collects Elves looks at him, then me. 'Who won in your game?'

Jonathan says nothing so I say that I did.

The twin slaps me on the shoulder. 'Good work man.'

Yes, I think. It was good work. I did everything right, for once, and now it was being ruined by Jonathan.

I go inside to get away. At the bar I see the Silvan Creatures player standing on her own. 'Let me get you a drink,' I say.

'Why don't you have a drink? Do you want a drink?'

'No,' she says.

I am a little flummoxed. Social situations are tough. I ask her about her last game and she says it was okay. She does not ask me back but I tell her I won. Talking about the game makes me feel I have won all over again and because she does not know Jonathan I do not have to think about how I won.

Once I have my drink I feel uncomfortable, like I do not have a reason to be at the bar. I nod towards the door. 'I should go.'

She dips her head. 'Cool meeting you.'

When it is time to leave, Jonathan goes ahead and climbs into the twins' car, slamming the door. I see through the dark glass of the window that he has put his miniature case on my seat, so I turn and go over to Dave's car.

Simon and Bryce talk continuously all the way out of Cardiff. It is not clear if they are listening to each other. Sometimes Dave guffaws but mostly he concentrates on driving. He drives slower than the twin who collects Undead and changes lanes less frequently.

Simon cannot get over how close he came to beating one of the Spanish players. 'I can't get over it,' he says. 'War machine and flyer combos. That's how you crack the Spanish meta. I'm gonna' write a post about it.' He twists in his seat to give us a crooked smile. 'I had him just where I wanted. Another turn and I would have won.' He points at me. 'It's all because of that game we played. That's why I took the Bolt Throwers. I put them in the centre like this, right?' He moves his hands around in the air to describe the positions of the units. When he is done explaining the battle he turns back in his seat and punches the palm of his hand. 'Fuck I want to play again.' He stares out the front window watching the white markings on the road race up and under us. After a while he says, 'Do you guys get that? You want to play again?'

'It certainly leaves you wanting more.' Dave speaks slowly, his eyes on the wing mirror. When he has changed lanes he pushes himself back against the seat. 'I still haven't worked out how to use those Mounted Sergeants.'

'No way do I want that to be my last game,' Bryce says. 'But where we going to play?'

No one replies. I roll my hoodie into a pillow and rest my head against it. It seems impossible that we will never play again but there it is. Not without the club and without the twin who collects Elves.

The suspension bridge towers rise up before us, spindly sans serif letters marked against the red brown banks of clouds. I play over that final game in my head: the echelon deployment, the peel charge, the Relic. Would I have won if I let him move his Relic? Was the peel charge enough? Maybe if he was actually my friend, I think, I should not have been such a douche.

THE SIEGE

I think about Jonathan a lot over the following weeks. Partly it is because we are not going to the club and I miss him but also it is because of the argument. It is this open-ended thing between us, something crooked that will keep unsettling me until it is straightened out. In the end I send him a picture of a Treeherder I have painted with the caption, 'Last march of the ents!' He does not reply, which makes me feel worse than before so I send him another message, asking how his Dwarf Goldpanners are coming along and again he does not reply. I have never known Jonathan not to reply to a message about Dwarves so I know something is up and that makes me feel worse than ever.

After two months of this, I get a little desperate and message the group. 'Does anyone want to play at that hipster bar that's reopened?' It is the last place I want to play but I remember Jonathan did not seem to mind.

Bryce replies saying, 'Fuck that shit.' And Simon sends an emoji of a skull and a wave, which I suppose means he thinks the idea is dead in the water. I get the sense Simon and Bryce are playing at Bryce's house and not inviting the rest of us.

The twin who collects Undead says we have no scenery anyway and the twin who collects Elves sends a picture of his baby, which is smaller, redder and more wrinkled than I think babies should be. Jonathan does not reply.

I think that is the end of it. I feel very low about the whole thing.

But a few days later the thread sparks up again when Simon suggests playing at a club in Lambeth. Bryce is up for it but Dave and the twin who collects Undead say it is too far.

Dave says we can play in his garage if he gets round to clearing it out, but none of us believe him. He has been meaning to clear it out for as long as we have known him. The thread falls silent again.

One day Dave messages to say he has found a miniature castle in his attic when rooting around for some LED bulbs and it seems crazy not to use it at least once.

I point out that now at least we have scenery and ask again if anyone is up for playing at the hipster bar. I am not usually this active in the group. Me and Jonathan are the same like that. We stay quiet until everyone has agreed on something. I keep checking my phone but no one responds all day. Then sometime in the evening, the twin who collects Undead says he is in. Once the twin who collects Undead is in, Simon and Bryce say they are up for it as well. The following morning, Jonathan messages, 'All right.'

I have hidden my miniature case inside a Bag for Life but I probably still look suspicious because who takes a Bag for Life into a bar? I suggested meeting early so the bar would be emptier but it is already pretty full with people having coffees and brunches. There is a spiral staircase in the far corner and I make for that. The tables they have reserved for us are on the first floor. Some people stare at me gormlessly and then back at their phones.

I have been anxious about seeing Jonathan but it is obvious from the moment I turn up that he wants to pretend everything is okay between us.

Dave has assumed the role of Games Master and has printed off the rules appendix on sieges. Attacking the castle would be the forces of evil, so Simon's Daemons, Bryce's Orcs and the twin's Undead. Defending it would be the forces of good, so my Halflings, Jonathan's Dwarves and Dave's Humans.

It takes a long time to set up for the siege game. Not only do we have to set up the castle, but we keep asking questions about siege rules and each time Dave has to look the answer up in the appendix. We miss the twin who collects Elves at that point. He would have learnt all the rules for us. But when it is finally set up it does look impressive. From our side of the table, it seems we are inside the castle looking out at the long lines of Daemons, Orcs and Undead massing on the far side of the valley. And when I go round to the other side and squat so my eye is at table level, the castle walls rear up darkly and I can make out the yellow and blue feathers in the helmets of Dave's arquebusiers and the silver blades of my Halfling Spearlings poking above the ramparts.

I go downstairs after the first turn to get a round of drinks. I have to queue for a while because the bar has filled up. The music is loud and people are spread over the terrace picnic tables. I am relieved to get back upstairs. When I give Jonathan his drink, I am hoping it will make me feel better, but it does not. I am not comfortable with the fact there is something unsaid between us but at the same time I cannot bring myself to say anything directly.

On their second turn Simon flies his Witch Queen on Giant Harpy inside the castle walls. We know it is going to happen but we are still unsure what to do about it. In the end Jonathan turns his cannons round and shoots her from the battlements. She dies but Simon grins when he removes her from the table so perhaps that is what he wanted to happen. We could have used the cannons to shoot the battering ram, which is rolling ever closer to the main gate. One of the hipsters comes up from downstairs and looks around as if he is unsure whether this is a private event, before going downstairs again.

On the third turn the battering ram takes down the gate. We were hoping it would survive at least a turn but Bryce rolls double six for damage.

Simon slaps his fingers and tells us we are fracking dead. He drains his pint and goes downstairs to get everyone a round.

In the break, Jonathan turns away from me and chats with Dave. For all his pretending that everything is okay, it is obviously not. I feel spare and self-conscious. I root around in my Bag for Life for the books that the twin who collects Undead lent me and go round the other side of the table to give them back.

I have thought a lot about that Nietzsche line and I think I do actually know what Gandalf would say. I think he would say that even the smallest person can change the fate of the world. Which is another way of saying that even the smallest person has power, that no one is such a weakling that their morality is never tested.

Simon comes back without drinks and rummages in his jacket for something. 'They fracking ID'd me.'

'It's 'cause you look so fresh bro,' Bryce says and the twin who collects Undead laughs.

It feels like they are having more fun on that side of the table. Jonathan is being uncharacteristically quiet but I am not sure what to do about it. To make it worse the music downstairs is getting louder and groups of people are starting to come upstairs to sit on the first floor terrace which is still in the sun. I can see them draped over the picnic tables, arching their heads back to blow smoke straight up in the air.

On the fourth turn Bryce's Orcs pour through the destroyed gate. Our first unit behind the gate is Jonathans' Dwarf Shieldwall company which we reckon can hold for a turn. But then Simon flies his Sorceress on Manticore over the wall to threaten their flank. Something needs to throw itself in between the Manticore and the Shieldwall company.

Jonathan sighs. 'I could move my Relic there.'

'No.' I say it louder than I expect. 'Keep the Relic back. I'll fly my Cockagriff in there.'

He studies the table for a moment. 'Really?'

'Yeah.' And because I really do want to clear the air I add, 'I definitely owe you a Relic.'

Jonathan does not reply but he raps the table with his knuckles and says, 'The game's afoot.'

On the fifth turn the Manticore kills the Cockagriff but the distraction works and the Shieldwall company holds. There is no time to celebrate though because that same turn, Bryce's Ogres destroy one of the wall sections and his units come pushing through the gap. Jonathan grips my shoulder and says, 'What new devilry is this!' And I know we are okay again.

Dave goes down to get us more beers. I realise I am quite drunk. We started early and now it is late afternoon. Most of the tables are full of people drinking and chatting. No one else is playing games. People stand round the edge of the room, resting their drinks on the thin shelf lining the wall, talking among themselves and watching us absently. I miss the club. I wonder if the Japanese students have found somewhere quiet to play Magic the Gathering.

A guy with a trapper hat saunters over and peers at my miniatures. He turns to me with a confused expression. 'What's going on?'

'It's a tabletop game,' I say. 'You measure things and roll dice.'

'You paint them as well?' He leans on his knees and peers at my Pony Riders. I pick them up and pass them to him and he turns them this way and that. 'You did the fucking eyeballs.' It is a neutral comment, but I am drunk and I feel good about how things have gone with Jonathan, so I decide to take it as a compliment.

There is a bartender moving between the tables collecting glasses. He comes towards us. We do not have any empty glasses. Maybe he is going to ask us to leave? Maybe we are not supposed to be here after all?

He looks at the miniatures. 'Who's winning lads?'

'Ah, it's too close to call,' Dave gestures towards the broken wall section and seems about to say more.

'Nice,' the bartender interrupts him. I realise he was only being polite. 'Look, no worries about the table. The DJ set doesn't start till eight.' He smiles broadly and moves away.

Jonathan nudges me but I do not understand why.

'What?'

He raises his eyebrows. 'The arrogance of the gift-giver!'

On the sixth and last turn all their units charge into our last line of defence around the keep: my Halfling Spearlings, Dave's Polearms and Jonathan's Relic. The game is on a knife edge. If we can somehow hold the line this turn and prevent them from entering the keep, we will win. There is something, as Jonathan would say, giddy-making about that.

My Spearlings and Dave's Polearms both die instantly. Simon, Bryce and the twin who collects Undead direct their remaining sixty-eight attacks against the Relic. We do not have enough dice so Simon rolls them in batches. Each time he is about to roll, Bryce, Jonathan and Dave drum on the table with their hands. Even the twin who collects Undead, who usually stands a few feet away from the table as if he is not with us, leans forward, biting his knuckle. What with all the drumming and Simon cackling and Dave groaning dramatically, a lot of people stop what they are doing and gather in a loose circle around us. They squint at the table and look from one to the other with bewildered expressions.

Of those sixty-eight attacks, they hit with thirty-two and wound with eighteen. The Relic has a courage of twenty so Jonathan has to roll no more than a total of two on two dice in order for the Relic to hold. There is only a one in thirty-six chance of rolling a double one. Still at these moments a tiny part of me always thinks that, somehow, it might just happen.

It is the deciding roll of the game, so we clear some space in the centre of the table. Jonathan makes a cage with his hands and shakes the dice energetically, first to one side of his head and then to the other. He is a dramatic roller. Then he holds his hands in front of his lips and says, 'By the Bones of the First Brewmaster of Stonehaven!' And rolls.

We all lean forward over the table to see the result. In fact everyone strains forward to see, even the people standing around us who have no idea what it means.

Acknowledgements

Thanks to Guy Harper-Day, this story's most ardent champion and guiding light.

Thanks to the writers of my workshop, Annie Bayley, Annie Fatet, Charlotte Barrow, Charlotte Reid, Jo Bedingfield, Joe Rizzo-Naudi, John Wilks, Laura Martz, Lake Wallis, Nick Burbidge, Nicola Brittain and Winnie M Li for their careful edits and ongoing support.

And thanks to Antigoni, for helping me solve all mysteries, plot related and otherwise.